Reading is the pathway
From the dungeon
To the door

Freedom

Reading is the highway from
The shadow to the sun

Freedom

Reading is the river
To your liberty
For all your life to come

Let the river run

Learn

Learn to read.

—MAYA ANGELOU

READ AND RISE

by Sandra L. Pinkney ✷ Photographs by Myles C. Pinkney

Foreword by Maya Angelou

SCHOLASTIC INC.
New York Toronto London Auckland Sydney Mexico City New Delhi Hong Kong

On Grandpa's lap
in a rocking chair
in search of land
exploring new worlds

Under the covers
flashlight in hand
having a wild adventure
spying tigers

In Daddy's chair
turning pages
looking out the cockpit
flying high in the sky

Sitting by the fire
in my mother's arms
with tape and bandages
healing all the hurts

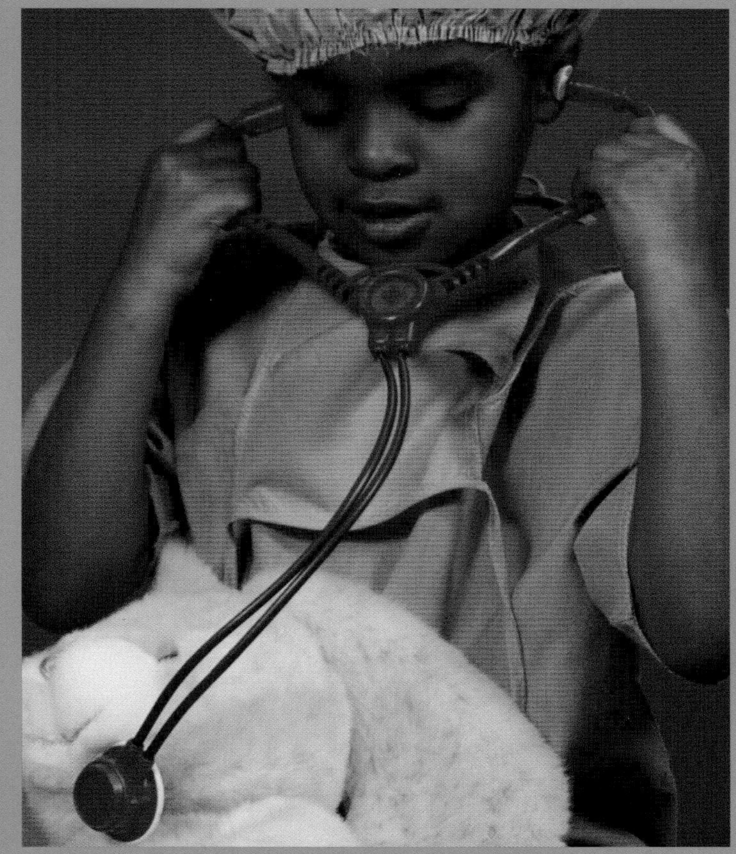

READ AND RISE

In the kitchen
on a stool
following a recipe
creating a delicious meal

In my bedroom
on the floor
surrounded by students
teaching them to read

At the schoolhouse
in a circle
shooting for the stars
soaring through space

Inside the library
lost in a book
putting out fires
rescuing people

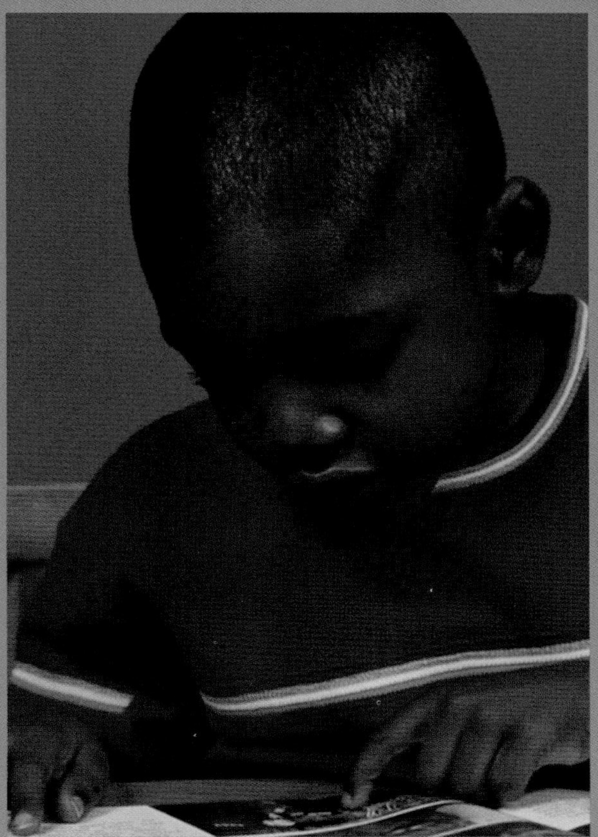

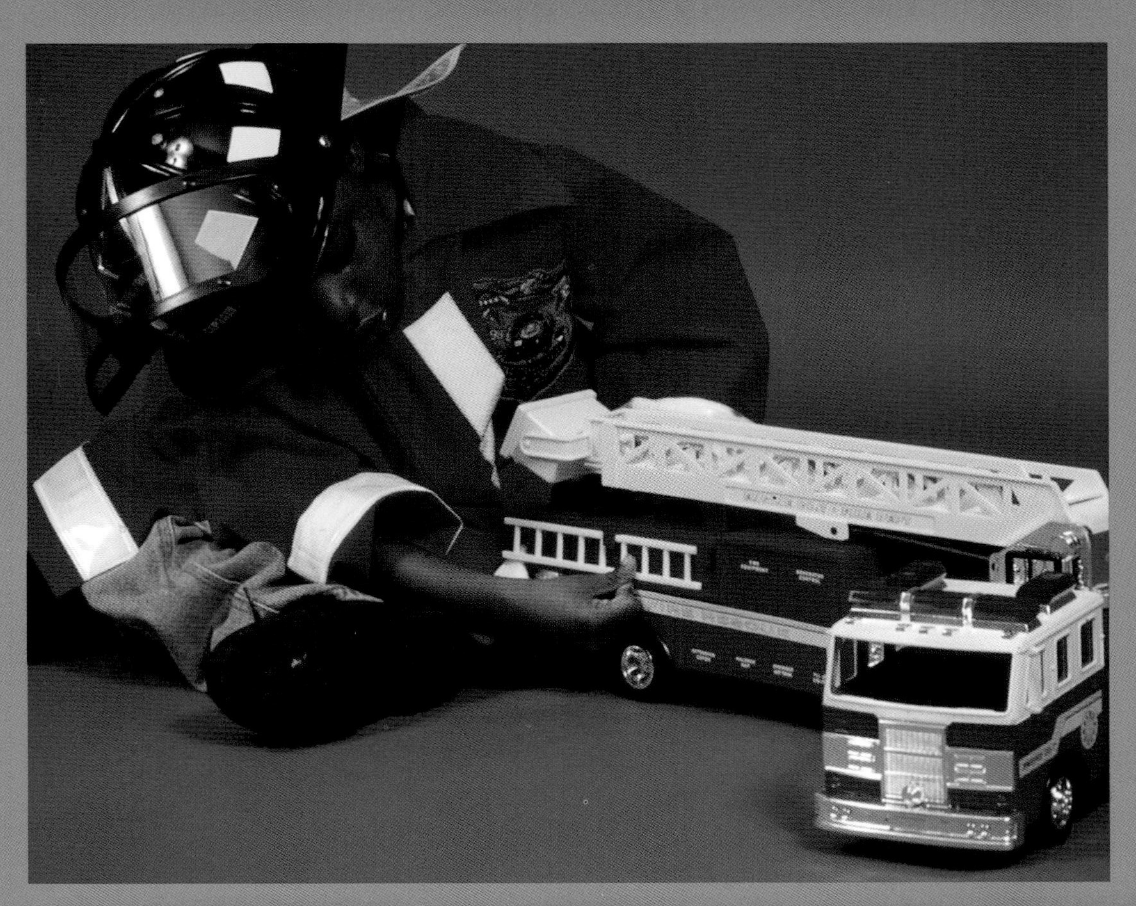

Read and Rise

At the park
on a bench
pitcher in motion
catching the action

On the couch
sister by my side
spinning and twirling
dancing on stage

Exploring

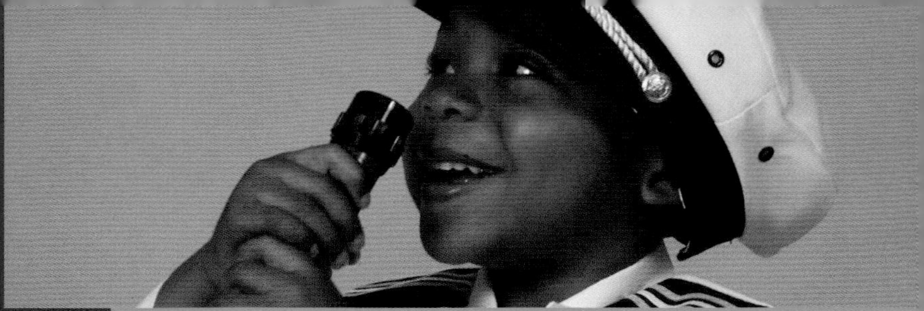

Spying

Flying

Healing

Cooking

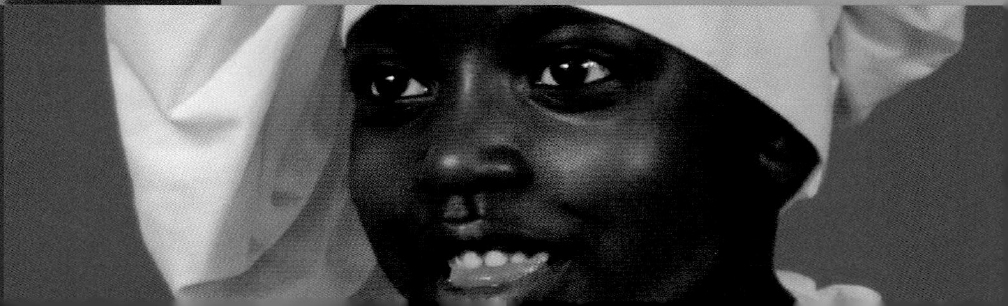

Teaching

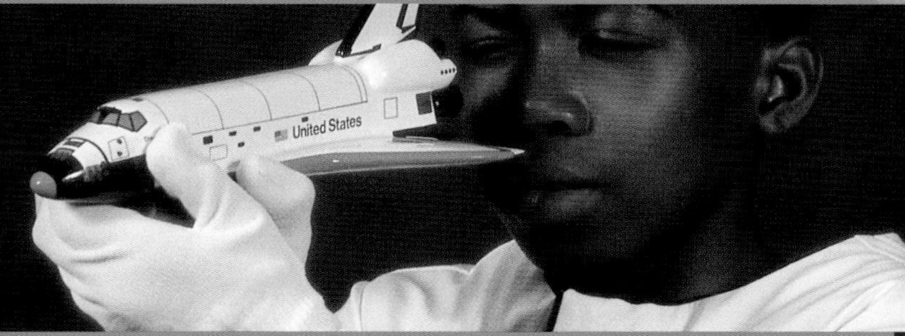

Soaring

Rescuing

Catching

Dancing

Just open a book to—

READ AND RISE

About the READ AND RISE Initiative

The National Urban League is the nation's oldest and largest movement to empower African-Americans to enter into the economic and social majority. In 1910, the founding of the Urban League began uniting affiliates in more than 100 cities all over the country. Through advocacy, research, community mobilization, partnerships, and policy analysis, the Urban League works to instill its message at local, state, and national levels.

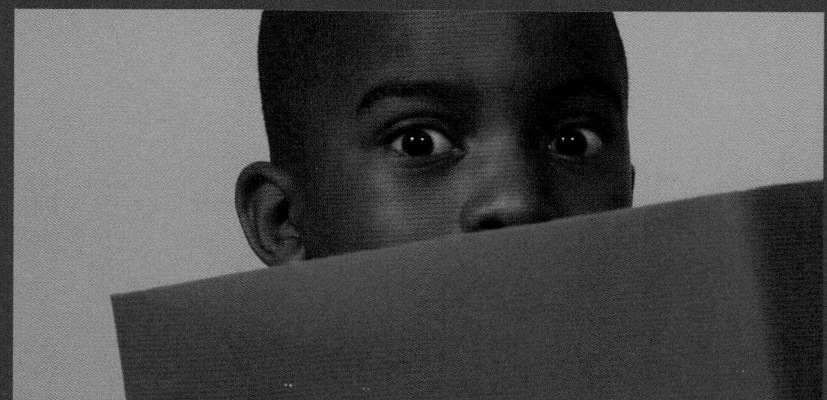

Scholastic Inc. has long recognized the need for commitment to public, private, and nonprofit organizations in order to promote reading and child literacy. In July 2001, Scholastic and the National Urban League launched a public service campaign intended to promote the power of reading to the African-American community. This collaboration produced ***Read and Rise: Preparing Our Children for a Lifetime of Success,*** a parents' guide to fostering reading skills in their children.

Since the launch of this campaign, Scholastic, the National Urban League, and Urban League affiliates and partners have spread the Read and Rise message by distributing more than one million guides, spearheaded a national public service radio campaign, and hosted Read and Rise Reading Circle (parent workshops) in communities across the country.

Read and Rise, by the award-winning team of author Sandra L. Pinkney and illustrator Myles C. Pinkney, is the newest addition to the Read and Rise initiative.

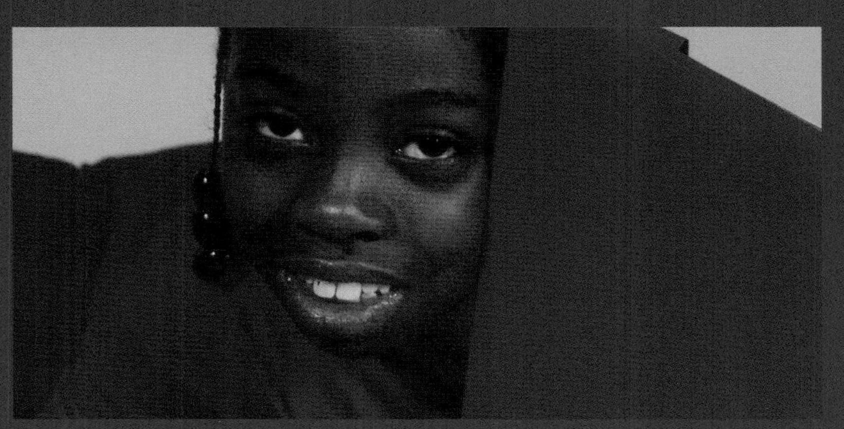

. . . Reading is the river
To your liberty
For all your life to come

Let the river run
Learn
Learn to read.

—MAYA ANGELOU

This book is dedicated to all the children who love to read, the families that read together, and all the children who want to become something great.

We would also like to thank all the children and families that participated in Read and Rise.

Special thanks to Principal Jackson-Ivey and the children of Clinton Elementary School, Poughkeepsie, New York.

—Myles and Sandra

Library of Congress Cataloging-in-Publication Data is available.

ISBN 0-439-30929-8

10 9 8 7 6 5 4 3 2 1 06 07 08 09 10

Printed in Singapore 46
First printing, January 2006

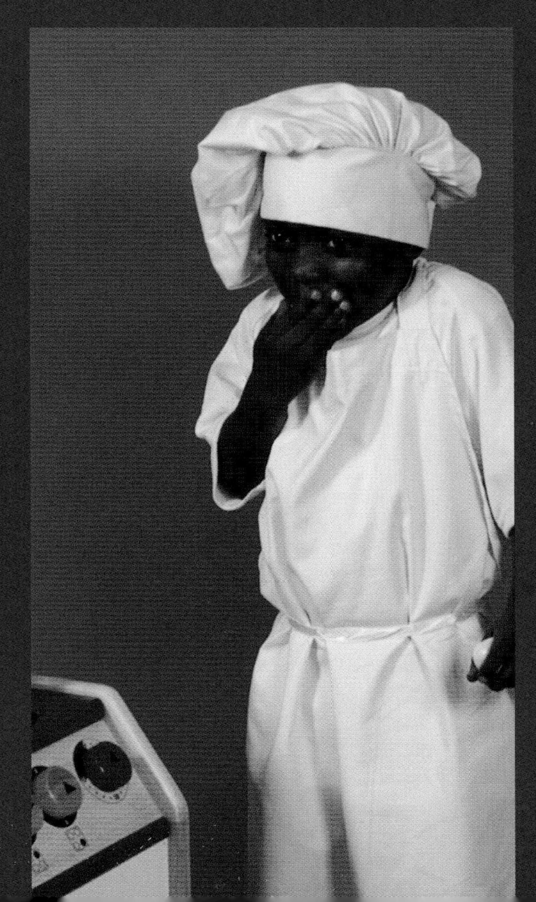

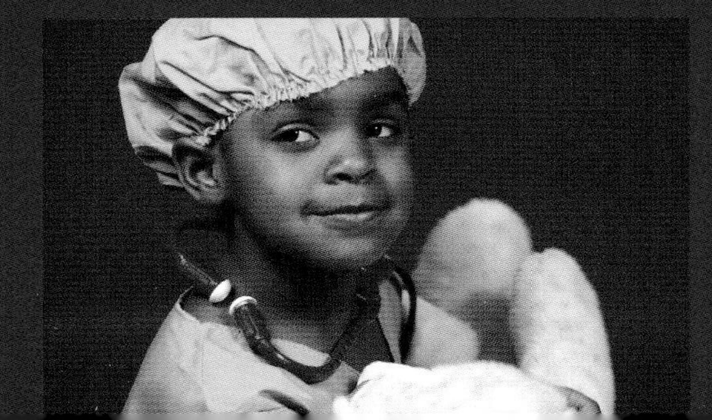